MATT CHRISTOPHER

MAN OUT AT FIRST

ILLUSTRATED BY ELLEN BEIER

NORWOOD HOUSE PRESS
CHICAGO, ILLINOIS

To Kimberley Marie, Evan Andrew, Paul Michael, and Julia Catherine

Norwood House Press
P.O. Box 316598
Chicago, Illinois 60631

For information regarding Norwood House Press, please visit our website at www.norwoodhousepress.com or call 866-565-2900.

This library edition was published in 2010.

Library of Congress Cataloging-in-Publication Data
Christopher, Matt.
   Man out at first / by Matt Christopher ; illustrated by Ellen Beier. — Library ed.
      p. cm. — (The new Peach Street Mudders library)
   Summary: After he gets hit by a fast-moving ball, Turtleneck Jones loses his confidence on the baseball diamond and sees his position at first base given to another player.
   ISBN-13: 978-1-59953-319-3 (library edition : alk. paper)
   ISBN-10: 1-59953-319-7 (library edition : alk. paper) [1.
Baseball—Fiction. 2. Self-confidence—Fiction.] I. Beier, Ellen, ill. II. Title.
   PZ7.C458Man 2009
   [Fic]—dc22   2009007923

Manufactured in the United States of America in North Mankato, Minnesota.
                                 166R—112010

1

"Wish me luck, Mom!" Turtleneck Jones called as he headed toward the door.

"Good luck, tall guy!" Mrs. Jones called back.

Turtleneck grinned. His mom always said that just before he went out to play baseball. He *was* tall for an eight-year-old. That's why Coach Parker had him play first base for the Peach Street Mudders.

He grabbed his glove and ran outside. At this time of year, nothing in this world was better than playing baseball!

He had just stepped off the porch when he heard a moan from the house next door. He looked over and saw his neighbor, Mr. Ebenezer Shaw, clutching his leg in pain.

"Wait a minute, Mr. Shaw!" Turtleneck cried. "I'll be right there!"

He rattled down the remaining steps and rushed next door. He saw the problem right away. Mr. Shaw's foot had fallen through a rotten part of his porch steps.

"Doggone step!" Mr. Shaw grunted. "Been meaning to fix it, but kept putting it off . . . putting it off. You should always take care of problems right away, Theodore."

"I guess so," Turtleneck said. He bent down to knock some of the broken pieces of wood aside so that Mr. Shaw could pull out his leg.

After a few minutes the old man's foot was free. Turtleneck helped him into the house. The Peach Street Mudders were playing the Joy Street Devils that afternoon and he didn't

want to be late. Coach Parker didn't tolerate lateness. But Turtleneck had to make sure Mr. Shaw was okay before he headed to the baseball diamond.

"Thanks, Theodore," Mr. Shaw said as he sat down in an easy chair and leaned his white cane against his leg. "I might have been stuck there all afternoon if you hadn't come along."

Turtleneck wondered why Mr. Shaw, a blind man, would want to live all by himself in this big, old house. Turtleneck's mom had told him that Mr. Shaw was very independent. But it was dangerous, Turtleneck thought.

Turtleneck bent down to give Mr. Shaw's foot a good look. "I don't see any bleeding or swelling, Mr. Shaw. Does anything hurt?"

"Nah." Mr. Shaw waved his hand. "I feel fine. Just a bit foolish." He pointed toward his wall of books. "Those books have taught me how to fix things, like leaky sinks and broken toasters." Mr. Shaw laughed. "Looks like I'll have to re-read the one on how to fix porch steps! Maybe you'd like to help me repair that hole?"

"I don't really know that much about carpentry, but I'll try," Turtleneck said. Then he glanced up at the clock on the wall. "Yikes!" He quickly jumped to his feet and grabbed his glove.

"I'm going to be late for my baseball game, Mr. Shaw! See you later!"

2

Turtleneck ran all the way to the baseball field. By the time he got there, the game had already started.

Coach Parker was sitting at the end of the dugout with the substitute members of the team. The rest of the Peach Street Mudders were out on the field. Turtleneck went over to apologize. "Sorry, Coach. I—I had to help a guy. His foot was stuck."

The coach looked at him with a raised eyebrow. "That's a new one. Grab some pine, T."

Turtleneck sat down next to Tootsie Malone, the outfield substitute, and looked at the scoreboard. It was already the bottom of the first inning. Then he glanced at the field and saw men on second and third.

"There's only one out so far. And they've already got one run," Tootsie said. "Jake Avery belted a homer."

"Rats," said Turtleneck. Jake Avery was the Joy Street Devils' leadoff hitter.

Sitting on the bench was a pain. Turtleneck could remember a time not too long ago when he sat on the bench more often than he played. New guys on a team—especially if they didn't have much experience—had to expect that. The better players always started first, then were replaced after three or four innings, provided there were enough subs to replace them.

Sparrow Fisher, the Mudders' left-handed pitcher, threw three strikes to Phil Hanson for the second out. Then little Sammy McFall hit

a pop-up to third base.

One inning was over and the Joy Street Devils led, 1–0.

Leading off for the Mudders was T.V. Adams. The husky third baseman had a knack for guessing where a lot of the opposing batters would hit a pitch. Turtleneck hoped T.V. would come up with a good hit himself this time.

"Strike!" yelled the ump.

Then *crack!* T.V. sent the ball soaring into left center field. He ran past first base, then stopped at second for a double.

Nick Chong got on first base when the Devils' shortstop missed a hot grounder. T.V. ran to third. He was in a good spot to score and tie the game.

But he never did. Alfie Maples popped up to the pitcher and Bus Mercer struck out. Rudy Calhoun walked to load the bases, but Sparrow grounded out to end the half inning.

The Joy Street Devils' fans cheered and whistled.

Turtleneck hoped the coach would tell him to take Bob Lopine's place at first. But the coach just yelled to the team to get out there and "play some heads-up ball!"

He's probably forgotten that I'm here, Turtleneck thought. Why did Mr. Shaw have to get his foot caught in that rotten old step, anyway?

The Devils' Frankie Bass blasted the first pitch for a double. Then Stretch Cantor hit a single through second and Frankie slid into home for another run. Reggie Mize flied out to left field. Two more singles resulted in another run before the Mudders could get the Devils out. Joy Street Devils 3, Peach Street Mudders 0.

At the top of the third, Barry "hit-away kid" McGee, the Mudders' best hitter, walloped a double over the shortstop's head. José Mendez stepped into the batter's box and Bob

Lopine took his place in the warm-up area. José took two strikes and then hit a double, an unusual thing for him. Barry made it home. Devils 3, Mudders 1.

I might as well have stayed home, Turtleneck thought.

Then he heard someone call his name.

3

"Turtleneck!" Coach Parker called again. "You're pinch-hitting for Bob."

"You heard him, Turtleneck," said Nick Chong, grinning. "Get a hit up there, okay?"

Turtleneck grabbed a bat and warmed up.

"Hey, Turtleneck! Think quick!" Nick called.

Turtleneck spun around quickly. He reached out his hands just in time to catch the batting helmet Nick had tossed to him. He grinned at Nick and put the helmet on.

Then he stepped into the batter's box. He

took two strikes, stepped out of the box for a few seconds, then took two balls.

The next pitch was right down the middle. *Crack!* Turtleneck sent the ball soaring to right center field. He raced around the bases for a stand-up triple. His heart pounded with joy.

José had made it home on Turtleneck's triple. The Mudders were only one run behind.

"Hey, man! You did it!" Nick called out to Turtleneck.

Rudy echoed, "Yeah, good thing you showed up today!"

"I didn't know you had it in you, T!" Bus Mercer yelled. "You're full of surprises today, aren't you?"

Yeah, thought Turtleneck. Now if T.V. can only knock me home!

T.V. did just that with a line drive between first and second.

As he sat down, Turtleneck could hear the Mudders' fans cheering and whistling.

He turned his attention back to the game and saw Nick Chong and Alfie both strike out. A pop-up by Bus Mercer ended the Mudders' turn at bat. The score was tied, 3–3.

At a nod from Coach Parker, Turtleneck grabbed his glove and headed out to first base. He felt good as he warmed up with the rest of the infield.

Barry McGee caught a long fly ball for the first out. Then little Sammy McFall walked. Man on first, one out.

Frankie Bass hit a dribbler to Sparrow. Sparrow scooped it up and quickly tossed it to Bus covering second.

Sammy was out, but Frankie, a fast runner, had almost made it to first. Turtleneck lowered his glove and waited for the next batter.

Then, out of the corner of his eye, he caught a blur of motion.

A split second later, a fast-moving baseball smacked hard into Turtleneck's chest!

Pain shot through him as he staggered back. For a moment he couldn't breathe. He heard yells and gasps from the fans.

All of a sudden, everything seemed to go black.

4

"Turtleneck? Can you hear me, son?"

Turtleneck opened his eyes slowly. He looked up into the worried face of Coach Parker. He struggled to get to his feet.

"Whoa there. Just take your time now," Coach warned.

He helped Turtleneck over to the dugout. "You look a little better, T, but I think you'd better grab a seat for now." He handed him an ice pack. "Here, put this on your chest. The cold will keep the swelling down."

Bus Mercer pounded his fist into his glove and walked out of the dugout. The rest of the team shuffled their feet as they looked at Turtleneck. None of them had ever seen anyone pass out before.

Turtleneck felt his face turn red. What a dope I am! he thought. Only 'fraidy cats faint!

Still, the memory of the baseball hitting his chest made him feel sick. It hurt a bit when he breathed in, too. He leaned back against the dugout wall and held the ice pack to his front.

Coach Parker gave Turtleneck one last look over, then yelled, "Play ball!" Jack Livingston, one of the regular infield subs, ran to cover first base.

Turtleneck squirmed uneasily on the bench. He wanted to be back in the game more than anything, but it was too late now. He didn't have a second chance. Not today. He'd not only been late to the game, he'd been benched after his first play in the field.

I should have known Bus would try for the double play, Turtleneck thought. I should have waited to see him toss the ball back to Sparrow. Now I'm back on the bench again. I wonder if the guys think this is where I should stay for good.

Turtleneck watched Bus throw the ball to Jack for an easy out at first. The inning ended with the score still 3–3.

Rudy Calhoun was up first for the Mudders at the top of fourth. He was also the first out.

Sparrow took two balls, then hit a single over the shortstop's head. The Devils' pitcher walked Barry McGee. Then José Mendez struck out. Two outs, two men on.

Jack Livingston stepped to the plate. He let the first pitch go by for a ball. Then he clobbered the second pitch for a double into right field. Both Sparrow and Barry scored. Cheers rose up from the Mudders' fans. Jack brushed the dirt from his pants and grinned.

Turtleneck watched the scorekeeper change the number beside the Mudders' name from 3 to 5 and grinned, too.

Coach Parker has to like that! he thought.

Then he had another thought. What if Coach Parker thinks Jack is good enough to replace me for the rest of the season?

Turtleneck's thoughts were interrupted when T.V. struck out, ending the inning.

The Joy Street Devils were two runs behind and seemed to be losing steam. Their first three batters went down swinging to end the fifth inning.

The Mudders didn't do much better. Nick popped out, and Alfie ticked two foul balls, then struck out.

Then Bus hit a line drive straight at the Devils' pitcher. But at the last second, the pitcher's glove shot up and he caught it for the last out.

The last inning was just as uneventful, and

the game ended happily for the Mudders. Final score, Mudders 5, Devils 3.

Turtleneck rose slowly from the bench. Well, at least my goof-up didn't keep us from winning, he thought with a sigh.

Still, he wanted to apologize to Bus for having muffed the double play. He glanced around and saw Bus strapping his glove to his bicycle rack. Turtleneck started toward him.

But before he took two steps, Nick and Rudy called over to him. They wanted to know what had made him faint.

"I thought that only happened if you saw a ghost," joked Nick.

"Yeah," Rudy joined in. "Or did you get frightened by a mouse, T?"

"Aw, knock it off," mumbled Turtleneck. He tossed the ice pack into the trash and picked up his glove.

"Hey, Turtleneck! Think quick!"

Nick's call startled Turtleneck. Instead of spinning and catching whatever Nick was tossing to him, he threw up his hands and ducked. A piece of ice arced over his head and landed on the ground in front of him. The laughter he heard coming from behind him was cut short by Coach Parker.

"Okay, boys, that's enough. Turtleneck's had a hard day." To Turtleneck he said, "Come on, I'll give you a lift home. I want to let your mother know what happened."

As Turtleneck got into the coach's car, he saw Bus watching him. Turtleneck waved. Bus gave him a funny look and then hopped on his bike and pedaled away fast.

5

When Mrs. Jones heard what had happened, she insisted that Turtleneck go to bed immediately. She fixed him a light dinner and tucked him in when he was through eating.

Turtleneck had trouble falling asleep that night. He replayed the moment just before Bus threw the ball over and over—only, in his mind, he caught the ball and made the double play. He kept remembering Nick and Rudy's comments and the odd look on Bus's face after the game.

I guess I really let everyone down, he thought dismally. Finally, he fell asleep.

The next sound Turtleneck heard was his father's voice calling him to breakfast.

"I hear you got the wind knocked out of you yesterday, T," his father said when he entered the kitchen. "Bus Mercer must have some throwing arm! Does it hurt much?"

"Not anymore," Turtleneck replied with a yawn. He pointed to his chest. "But there's a big bruise right here." He poured himself a bowl of cereal and began eating.

The phone rang. Turtleneck answered it.

"Hi, Theodore, this is Mr. Shaw," said a familiar voice. "Feel up to learning a bit about carpentry this morning? I've decided to fix that step right away. Now that it's a hole instead of just a weak spot, it really needs to be taken care of."

"I've got baseball practice this morning. But I'll come over this afternoon if you want," Turtleneck replied.

"Thanks, Theodore. I knew I could count on you."

Turtleneck was just finishing his breakfast when the doorbell rang. When he opened the door, Nick Chong and Rudy Calhoun were waiting on the other side.

"Hey, Turtleneck! Ready to go to practice?" Rudy asked.

"We told the coach to get rid of all the ghosts and mice so you won't faint again today," Nick said.

Turtleneck felt his face turn red. These guys aren't ever going to let me live that down, he thought.

He got his glove and told his parents where he was going. The three boys headed for the diamond.

"You sure looked weird when you passed out yesterday," Nick said. "Your eyeballs went all funny and you just sort of fell over."

"Bus looked pretty funny, too! Like he couldn't believe you tried to catch the ball with your chest!'' Rudy laughed.

Turtleneck looked quickly at the two boys. I guess Bus does blame me for messing up the double play, he thought. He straightened his cap and added silently, Well, I guess I'll just have to show him—and Coach Parker—what I'm *really* made of!

Most of the team was already warming up by the time Turtleneck, Rudy, and Nick reached the baseball diamond. Jack Livingston was at first base. He stretched out his glove and caught a throw from Bus easily.

Coach Parker called Turtleneck over to him. ''You don't look any worse for your injury, T, but I'm going to keep Jack at first for now,'' he said. ''Run a couple laps around the field to warm up. Then you can hit some to the infield.''

The outfielders were already running around the outside of the field. Turtleneck joined them. He jogged slowly.

Coach Parker must be afraid I'll mess up

again, he thought dismally.

Turtleneck finished one loop around the outfield. He was about to begin another lap when Coach Parker called to him to pick up a bat.

"Okay, T, just knock in a few grounders for now. Run the bases, too. I want the infield to feel like it's a game situation."

Sparrow Fisher was on the mound. He wound up and threw a fast pitch. Turtleneck watched the ball come toward him—and suddenly he jumped back out of the batter's box. The ball just missed him.

"Sorry, T!" yelled Sparrow. "That one got away from me."

Shaken, Turtleneck stepped back into the box. His mind raced. What if that ball had hit me? he thought. Would I have fainted again? The guys would never stop razzing me if I did! And Coach won't keep a 'fraidy cat at first, that's for sure.

His mind racing, Turtleneck waited for the

next pitch. *Crack!* This time he swung hard and sent the ball soaring into left field. He felt great as he rounded first and headed for second.

Then his good mood vanished as quickly as it had come. He'd messed up again.

6

Coach had told him to hit easy grounders to the infield. Turtleneck looked to where he'd hit the ball. It lay way out in left field. No one was there to catch it. The outfielders were still doing laps.

Bus had to leave his position at shortstop to retrieve the ball.

"Nice hit, T," Bus said dryly. "Next time try hitting it to the *infield*." He threw the ball back to Sparrow.

Turtleneck felt awful. Even when I try not to, I mess up, he thought. He kicked at the dirt around second base.

Zero Ford, the substitute pitcher, was next at bat. He bunted. Sparrow Fisher charged in and scooped the ball up. He whipped it to Jack Livingston, but his throw was wild. Jack couldn't get a glove on it. Zero was safe at first.

Coach Parker called the outfield in to take their turns at bat. Barry McGee came to the plate.

"It'll be hard for me to keep the ball in the infield, but I'll see what I can do," he joked. Then he hit a hot grounder between second and third.

Turtleneck took off for third. T.V. rushed to cover the base. Bus Mercer ran to get in front of the ball before it rolled into the outfield.

T.V. stretched out his glove, his toe squarely on the bag. Turtleneck knew he'd have to put on a burst of speed to beat the ball. He heard Coach yelling for him to slide.

Turtleneck suddenly panicked. I'll run

smack into T.V. if I slide! he thought wildly. But maybe Bus's throw will hit me if I don't!

Turtleneck froze. *Thud!* The ball landed solidly in T.V.'s outstretched mitt. Turtleneck was out.

"What's the matter with you, T?" Bus asked. "Why didn't you slide?"

"Maybe he only remembers how to fall down, like he did yesterday!" T.V. said.

Coach Parker just shook his head and told Turtleneck to take Jack Livingston's place at first.

But things seemed to go from bad to worse. Every time a teammate tried to make a play at first, Turtleneck shied away from the ball. He spent more time chasing it after it flew past him than he did making outs.

By the time Jack took over at first again, Turtleneck was a wreck.

He wasn't much better at bat. Whenever a pitch looked a little wild, Turtleneck jumped out of the batter's box.

Finally, the practice was over. Coach Parker called the team together.

"We're playing the High Street Bunkers tomorrow. I expect to see all of you here bright and early. Here's the lineup. Outfield from left to right: Barry, José, and Alfie. Infield: T.V. at third, Bus at short, Nick at second, and Jack at first. Sparrow, you'll pitch, and Rudy will catch."

Turtleneck's heart sank. Just what he was afraid of—Coach was replacing him at first base.

7

Turtleneck was silent as he walked home with Rudy and Nick. He mumbled "See ya" to them when they reached their houses. Then he continued on alone to his house.

He was walking up to his front door when he heard Mr. Shaw call to him.

"That you, Theodore? Ready to take a stab at the old porch steps?"

Turtleneck was about to answer but then closed his mouth. He suddenly felt like shutting out the whole world.

Besides, he thought dully, I don't know anything about carpentry. I'd just get in the way. Or else I'd mess the whole thing up. Then Mr. Shaw could hurt himself again and it would be all my fault.

Mr. Shaw called again. "T? Are you there, son?" He sounded a little uncertain this time.

He doesn't know for sure that it's me, Turtleneck reminded himself, and I don't have to tell him.

As quietly as he could, Turtleneck opened the door to his house and slipped inside.

Turtleneck went to his room and lay on his bed. He picked up a comic book and started leafing through it. He heard the phone ring and his mother answer it.

"I think he's in his room, Mr. Shaw," his mother said. "Hold on and I'll check."

His mother opened his door. Turtleneck closed his eyes and pretended to be asleep.

"He must be worn out. He's fast asleep,"

his mother said into the phone. "It's not like Turtleneck to forget a promise. I'll send him over when he wakes up." She hung up.

A moment later, Turtleneck heard the sound of hammering coming from next door. It went on for a bit, then all of a sudden it stopped. Turtleneck got up quietly and peeked through the window.

Mr. Shaw seemed to be feeling around on the porch for something. "Doggone it!" Turtleneck heard him say. "Where did I put that tape measure?"

From where he was standing, Turtleneck could see the tape measure. It had fallen into the grass beside the porch.

Turtleneck felt awful. He had promised to help Mr. Shaw but had chickened out just because he was afraid of messing up!

I'm letting everybody down, he thought. No wonder Coach Parker put Jack in my place. He knows I'm just a big 'fraidy cat.

He lay back down on his bed again.

Turtleneck didn't realize he'd fallen asleep for real until he felt his mother shaking him awake.

"Mr. Shaw is here to see you, T."

Turtleneck sat up. Mr. Shaw came in and sat on the edge of his bed.

"Your mom told me about your injury yesterday, Theodore. It must still hurt a lot," he said.

Turtleneck didn't know what to say. "It— it's not so bad anymore, Mr. Shaw," he finally mumbled.

Mr. Shaw was quiet for a moment. Then he said, "Did you hear me calling you earlier today, Theodore?"

Turtleneck hung his head. "Yes," he whispered. There was no use in lying to Mr. Shaw. Even though he was blind, he seemed to see everything.

"Do you mind telling me why you didn't answer? And why you decided not to come over and help me?"

"I was afraid I'd mess things up!" Turtleneck burst out. Then he told him all about the horrible practice he'd had that day.

To his surprise, Mr. Shaw started laughing.

"When I heard you'd been hit, I figured it was something like that. I know exactly how you're feeling, Theodore. Things that once seemed easy now seem impossible—and anything new is too scary to try, right?"

"Right!" said Turtleneck, amazed. "How did you know?"

"I've had those same fears myself. And I can tell you that the only cure is to face them head on."

"I don't know . . ." said Turtleneck. "What if I get hit again?"

"Hey, if I had that kind of attitude, I'd be locked up in some nursing home. You've got to keep trying. The longer you put it off, the worse it'll get."

Turtleneck thought for a moment. Then he grinned. "You mean like that rotten old porch step?"

Mr. Shaw laughed again and rubbed his sore leg. "Exactly! Now what do you say we go and tackle that problem head on together?"

8

For the rest of the afternoon, Turtleneck helped Mr. Shaw rebuild his steps. He hammered a few nails in crooked by mistake, but most of them went in fine.

That night Turtleneck slept soundly. He woke up refreshed and ready for the game against the High Street Bunkers. He went to the kitchen and poured himself a big bowl of cereal. He flipped through his comic book as he ate.

Then he remembered that Jack Livingston was starting at first. And he remembered how lousy he'd played at practice.

Suddenly he wasn't so sure he wanted to go to the game after all.

He pushed his half-eaten bowl of cereal aside, grabbed his comic book, and went to sit on the front porch.

Superheroes flew and ran across the pages in front of him. *They* didn't look like they ever messed up or were afraid of anything.

Turtleneck heard a sound and looked up. Nick Chong and Rudy Calhoun were walking toward him. They were wearing their uniforms and carrying their gloves.

"Aren't you ready for the game, T?" Nick asked.

Turtleneck was silent for a moment. "Listen, guys, I'm—I'm not feeling very good. Could you tell Coach Parker I won't be able to make it today?"

Nick and Rudy stared at each other in amazement.

"But we're playing the High Street Bunkers today and we need you!" Rudy cried.

"Jack starts today. I'd just be sitting on the bench anyway," Turtleneck reminded him.

"Never mind," Nick cut in disgustedly. "Maybe Jack *will* come through. C'mon, we don't want to be late. Coach Parker might bench us, too."

He grabbed Rudy's arm and tugged him down the steps. The two boys walked away without a backward glance.

Turtleneck closed his comic book and watched his friends pass by Mr. Shaw's house.

I wonder if those guys even care if I play or not, he thought.

A flash of light from next door caught his eye. The sun was reflecting off one of the new nails he'd hammered into Mr. Shaw's steps.

Turtleneck looked at it for a moment. And suddenly he realized that *he* cared whether he played or not.

He jumped up and ran into the house. He quickly changed into his uniform, grabbed his glove, and headed out the door.

46

9

Turtleneck rattled down the steps and started off toward the baseball diamond. Then he stopped.

He ran up Mr. Shaw's steps and knocked at the door.

"Who is it?" a voice called from inside.

"It's me, Turtleneck, uh, Theodore," Turtleneck replied. He poked his head around the door and peered inside. Mr. Shaw was sitting in his easy chair, listening to music. "Would—would you come to my baseball game with me?"

Mr. Shaw grinned and snapped off the radio. "Best offer I've had all day!" he said.

By the time they made it to the baseball diamond, the game had already begun. Turtleneck helped Mr. Shaw find a seat, then ran over to the dugout.

Coach Parker looked surprised to see him.

"Rudy and Nick told me you weren't feeling well, T," he said. He raised an eyebrow. "Looks like you recovered. Grab some pine."

Turtleneck hesitated for a moment. The only open spot on the bench was next to Nick.

I wonder if he's still sore at me, Turtleneck thought.

As if he could read his thoughts, Nick looked up at Turtleneck and grinned. "I think I can squeeze you in over here," he joked as he pointed to the space beside him. "Glad you could make it, T."

Turtleneck sat down with a laugh and replied, "Well, *someone* has to get the chatter started." He cupped his hands around his mouth and yelled, "C'mon, Mudders!" The rest of the team echoed his cry with encouraging yells of their own.

The High Street Bunkers hadn't scored any runs in their turn at bat, so the score was still 0–0. T.V. Adams was up first for the Mudders in the bottom of the first inning. He faced Alec Frost, the Bunkers' pitcher. Alec had a fastball that could whiz by a batter in the wink of an eye.

But T.V.'s eyes never left the ball on the first pitch. He sent the ball flying far into the outfield for a solid single.

Nick Chong was the next batter. He took a couple of practice swings, then stepped into the batter's box. Alec's fastball sizzled toward him.

"Strike!" the umpire yelled.

"C'mon, Nick, you can do it!" Turtleneck cried.

Nick adjusted his batting helmet and got ready for the next pitch. *Crack!* He belted a hot grounder that advanced T.V. to second. Nick made it to first safely.

Alfie Maples, the quiet right fielder, took two balls, then popped out. Bus Mercer was up next. He looked ready for anything Alec Frost had up his sleeve.

Alec reared back and threw. A wild pitch! Bus barely had time to jump out of the way. After three more pitches, Bus walked.

Bases loaded and only one out. Rudy Calhoun stepped into the batter's box.

Three swings later he stepped out again. Two outs.

Rudy walked back to the dugout. Turtleneck punched him lightly in the shoulder.

"Shake it off, man," he said. "You'll get another chance to hit." But I wonder if *I'll* get a chance to hit this game, he added silently.

Rudy smiled weakly and turned to watch Sparrow Fisher bat.

Sparrow took his time waiting for the right

pitch. He took a ball and two strikes before he swung at the fourth pitch.

Crack! He hit a line drive between second and third. The ball just missed the shortstop's glove. T.V. made it home.

Mudders 1, Bunkers 0. Two out, bases loaded—and Barry McGee, the Mudders' strongest hitter, was at the plate.

Barry let the first pitch go by for a called strike. Then he swung with all his might at the second pitch. Bat connected with ball and sent it soaring over the outfielders' heads. A home run!

The Mudders' fans cheered loudly. Turtle-neck could hear Mr. Shaw yelling with the others.

José Mendez struck out to end the inning. Mudders 5, Bunkers 0.

The second, third, and fourth innings went scoreless for both teams. The Mudders were getting ready to take the field when Coach

Parker called Turtleneck and Jack Livingston over.

"Jack, you've played a good game," he said. "Now I'm going to give Turtleneck a chance. Don't let me down, T."

Turtleneck took a deep breath and replied, "I won't, Coach." To himself he added, *I hope.*

10

Turtleneck headed to first base. As he passed by the stands he saw that Mr. Shaw was smiling. I wonder if he knows I'm on the field, Turtleneck thought.

Then Mr. Shaw yelled, "C'mon, Theodore—Turtleneck! Show 'em what you're made of!"

Turtleneck pounded his fist into his glove. Okay, Mr. Shaw, he thought with determination. I'm going to do my best!

The infield threw the ball around the bases a few times to warm up. Turtleneck felt a little better each time the ball landed safely in his glove.

Sparrow Fisher hurled the first pitch. The batter belted a hot grounder straight to Bus and took off for first. Bus scooped up the ball. He turned and threw it hard to Turtleneck.

Turtleneck stretched out his glove. The ball zoomed toward him. Closer, closer—*thud!* He caught it in the webbing of his mitt for the first out.

Cheers rose from the stands. Turtleneck tossed the ball back to Sparrow. He glanced over at Bus. But Bus was already waiting for the next batter.

Is he still mad at me? Turtleneck wondered. Then he shrugged and got ready, too.

The second batter went down swinging, but the third slugged the ball into the outfield for a double. Two outs, and a man on second.

"Okay, team, here we go!" Coach Parker yelled from the dugout. "The throw goes to first for the last out! Let's make it count, now!"

Turtleneck had butterflies in his stomach.

What if he couldn't catch the throw?

Sparrow threw a fastball. The Bunkers' batter swung hard and sent the ball down the first-base line. Turtleneck reached his glove out to snag it.

The ball hit a stone and took a crazy bounce. It shot up toward his face! Turtleneck jerked his head to one side just before the ball hit him. It landed in the grass behind him. There was a groan from the crowd as he ran back to retrieve it. The batter was safe at first.

Turtleneck was shaken. How could he muff such an easy out? Worse yet, what would he have done if the ball had hit him?

Turtleneck's mind was racing. Then he heard a voice yelling his name.

"Turtleneck! Don't let it bother you! Shake it off, man!"

The voice belonged to Bus Mercer. Amazed, Turtleneck turned to look at him.

Bus was watching, concerned. When he

saw Turtleneck look over, he gave him the "thumbs up" sign. Then he turned his attention back to Sparrow.

Turtleneck didn't know what to think. Then he took a deep breath. He tried to take Bus's advice and "shake it off." He bent down and waited for Sparrow to pitch.

Crack! A line drive straight back at Sparrow! But instead of snagging the ball for the last out, Sparrow ducked. The ball flew over his head, took one hop, then landed smack in Nick Chong's glove.

Toe on the bag, Turtleneck reached out to catch Nick's throw. It came straight at him—fast.

Thud! Something hit him in the chest. For a split second Turtleneck thought he'd dropped the ball. Then he heard cheers. He looked down and saw he was cradling it in his glove against his chest.

Three outs and the Mudders were still up, 5–0.

The Mudders headed for the dugout. Turtleneck hesitated, then sat down between Bus and Nick in the dugout.

Bus was quiet for a second. Then he cleared his throat. "T, I feel awful about the other day. It was all my fault. I didn't look to see if you were ready to catch my throw—I just threw it." He dug his toe in the dirt. "I should have said something sooner. Are you feeling okay now?"

Before Turtleneck could answer, Sparrow came and sat next to Nick. "Great snag, Nick. You saved the play! I don't know what came over me. I saw that ball coming and I thought for sure it was going to hit me." He thumped Turtleneck on the back and grinned. "And we all know what happens when you get hit by a ball!"

Bus shot a sideways glance at Turtleneck.

Turtleneck was silent for a moment. Then, with a muffled laugh, he pretended to faint. He collapsed at Nick's feet and lay still.

Everyone started laughing. Coach Parker rushed over to see what was wrong. Turtleneck scrambled to his feet.

"Well, T, you certainly seem to be back into the swing of things. Now let's see if the swing is back in you!" He handed him a bat.

"Yes, sir!" said Turtleneck.

He trotted to the on-deck circle and took a few practice swings. He was just about to step into the batter's box when he heard a yell from behind him.

"Hey, Turtleneck! Think quick!"

Turtleneck dropped the bat and spun around quickly. He caught the protective helmet Nick had tossed to him. Nick laughed.

"Nice to have you back, T," he called from the dugout.

Turtleneck just grinned and picked up the bat.

Okay, Alec Frost, he said to himself. Throw that ball as hard as you can. I'm ready!

READ ALL THE BOOKS IN THE

THE NEW PEACH STREET MUDDERS LIBRARY!